Bella Up, Up, and Away

Copyright © 2016 by Ryan O'Rourke

All rights reserved. Manufactured in China.

www.harpercollinschildrens.com

Library of Congress Cataloging-in-Publication Data

O'Rourke, Ryan, author, illustrator.

    Bella up, up, and away / Ryan O'Rourke. — First edition.

        pages   cm

    Summary: When the life preserver her new friend Claude is napping on drifts out to sea, Bella the lighthouse cat finds the adventure she is seeking—and makes another new friend along the way.

    ISBN 978-0-06-221863-6 (hardcover)

    [1. Cats—Fiction.   2. Adventure and adventurers—Fiction.   3. Friendship—Fiction.   4. Dolphins—Fiction.]   I. Title.

PZ7.O655Bh 2015   2014005876

[E]—dc23   CIP

                                                                          AC

The artist used mixed media, hand lettering, and Photoshop to create the digital illustrations for this book.

Typography by Martha Rago

16 17 18 19 20 SCP 10 9 8 7 6 5 4 3 2 1

❖

First Edition

BELLA
Up, Up, and Away

Ryan O'Rourke

HARPER
An Imprint of HarperCollins Publishers

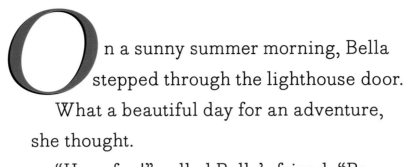

On a sunny summer morning, Bella stepped through the lighthouse door.

What a beautiful day for an adventure, she thought.

"Have fun!" called Bella's friend. "Be back in time for dinner!"

The little cat ran toward the seashore.

SN-O-O-ORE....

On her way to the shore, Bella passed by
a rosebush. She heard a sound in the thicket.
What could that be? she thought.

Yawn!

To Bella's surprise, a big, fluffy gray cat popped out of the rosebush!

"Hello there!" said the furry feline. "My name is Claude. I'm sorry if I startled you."

"Hello, I'm Bella. Would you like to go on an adventure?"

"That sounds delightful," said Claude.

Running ahead, Bella led her new companion to the water's edge.

Bella splashed into the surf. The curious kitty chased a school of fish.

Claude stayed on the shore. The sand was warm under his furry paws. The big cat sat and watched the shapes in the clouds.

"Let's build a sand castle!" said Bella. As she built her castle, she imagined she was a medieval knight defending her kingdom.

"I'd rather take a nap," said Claude.
The big gray tabby curled up in a life raft
he found and soon fell asleep.

While Bella daydreamed, her new friend had floated away!
Bella ran to the water's edge. She could hear Claude calling for
help. She could barely see him over the waves.

Bella didn't know what to do.

As she tried to think, a loud flock of seagulls soared above her.
A plan started to form in Bella's mind.

Bella found a kite in the sand.
That will do, she thought.

She held the spool
tightly in her mouth,

and the wind lifted Bella
up into the air!

Bella was flying!

Soon Bella spotted Claude sitting in the ocean.
"Claude!" called Bella.
But when the adventurous kitty called to Claude,
the spool fell out of her mouth. Bella was falling.

The little cat plunged into the sparkling blue water and bobbed back to the surface. Bella swam to Claude, who helped her climb into the life raft.

"Thanks!" said Bella. "I was trying to save *you*!"

The two cats sat together, surrounded by the ocean.

"I'm glad you're here," said Claude. "But how will we ever get home?"

Bella and Claude spotted a fin popping out of the water nearby.
They nervously watched as the fin came closer and closer until . . .

A dolphin sprang over their heads!

"You look like you could use a little help," said the dolphin.

"Can you help us get back to shore?" asked Bella.

"Of course!" said the dolphin.

Taking the rope from the life raft in his mouth, he began to tow the two cats.

HANG

Bella, Claude, and the dolphin dashed through the waves.
Soon Bella could see the lighthouse coming into view.

The dolphin towed the two cats all the way to the water's edge.

"Thanks for your help," said Bella and Claude.

"You're welcome!" said the dolphin. He called good-bye, then disappeared into the waves.

"All this excitement has made me
quite hungry," said Claude.
"Me too," said Bella. "Let's go eat!"
Bella and Claude scampered up the
hill to the lighthouse.

Bella thought happily about the day's adventure
and her new friend. She wondered if Claude would
want to come on her next adventure.
"Time for a nap," said Claude.
Maybe, thought Bella, or maybe not!

AMERICAN
CIVILIZATION

A PORTRAIT FROM

AMERICAN

TEXTS BY

EDITED BY DANIEL J. BOORSTIN

McGRAW-HILL BOOK COMPANY
NEW YORK